A
TREE
for ME

A TREE for ME

BY Nancy Van Laan

ILLUSTRATED BY Sheila White Samton

Alfred A. Knopf
New York

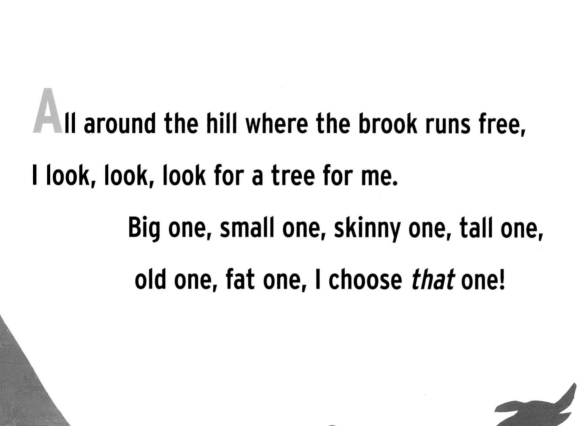

All around the hill where the brook runs free,

I look, look, look for a tree for me.

Big one, small one, skinny one, tall one,

old one, fat one, I choose *that* one!

Up I go to the tippy tiptop.

Uh-oh!

Oh, no!

Wait a minute. STOP!

I'm mistaken.

This one's taken.

One owl nesting,
golly gee!
No room for me
in this ol' tree.

All along the brook, frogs peep, "Chip-chee!"

as I look, look, look for a tree for me.

Big one, small one, skinny one, tall one,

old one, fat one, I choose *that* one!

Up I go to the tippy tiptop.

Uh-oh!

Oh, no!

Wait a minute. STOP!

I'm mistaken.

This one's taken.

Two possums dangling,
golly gee!
No room for me
in this ol' tree.

In the weeds, grasshoppers fiddle diddle dee
as I look, look, look for a tree for me.
Big one, small one, skinny one, tall one,
old one, fat one, I choose *that* one!

Up I go to the tippy tiptop.

Uh-oh!

Oh, no!

Wait a minute. STOP!

I'm mistaken.

This one's taken.

Three worms crawling,
golly gee!
No room for me
in this ol' tree.

By the pond, butterflies flit and flee

as I look, look, look for a tree for me.

Big one, small one, skinny one, tall one,

old one, fat one, I choose *that* one!

Up I go to the tippy tiptop.

Uh-oh!

Oh, no!

Wait a minute. STOP!

I'm mistaken.

This one's taken.

Four squirrels quarreling,
golly gee!
No room for me
in this ol' tree.

On moss-covered rocks, crickets chirp, "Chirree!"

as I look, look, look for a tree for me.

Big one, small one, skinny one, tall one,

old one, fat one, I choose *that* one!

Up I go to the tippy tiptop.

Uh-oh!

Oh, no!

Wait a minute. STOP!

I'm mistaken.

This one's taken.

Five spiders spinning,
golly gee!
No room for me
in this ol' tree.

Deep in the woods, I hear a chickadee

as I look, look, look for a tree for me.

Big one, small one, skinny one, tall one,

old one, fat one, I choose *that* one!

Up I go to the tippy tiptop.

I climb and climb and do not stop.

No owl nest, no possums rest,

no inchworms crawl,

no squirrels at all,

no spiders creep—

—just me, asleep.

Chip-chee, chirree,
fiddle dee,

Z Z Z Z Z Z.

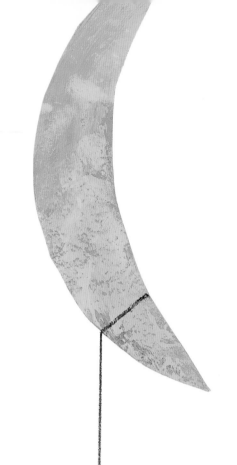

THIS IS A BORZOI BOOK PUBLISHED BY ALFRED A. KNOPF, INC.
KNOPF, BORZOI BOOKS, and the colophon are registered trademarks
of Random House, Inc.

Text copyright © 2000 by Nancy Van Laan
Illustrations copyright © 2000 by Sheila White Samton
All rights reserved under International and Pan-American Copyright Conventions.
Published in the United States of America by Alfred A. Knopf,
and simultaneously in Canada by Random House of Canada Limited, Toronto.
Distributed by Random House, Inc., New York.

www.randomhouse.com/kids

Library of Congress Cataloging-in-Publication Data
Van Laan, Nancy.
A tree for me / by Nancy Van Laan ; illustrated by Sheila White Samton.—1st ed.
p.   cm.
Summary: A child climbs five different trees, looking for a place to hide and
finding an increasing number of animals already in residence, until finally the
perfect tree is found.
[1.Trees—Fiction. 2. Animals—Fiction. 3. Counting. 4. Stories in rhyme.]
I. Samton, Sheila White, ill. II. Title.
PZ8.3.V34 Tr 2000
[E]—dc21   99-047440

ISBN 0-679-89384-9 (trade)
ISBN 0-679-99384-3 (lib. bdg.)

First Edition
March 2000
Printed in Hong Kong
10 9 8 7 6 5 4 3 2 1

For my cousin Jinny
N.V.L.

For Willa the Woo
S.W.S.